CW00537786
£4.99
UK only

CONTENTS

Created by: Britt Allcroft from the works of Katharine Tozer
Written by: Britt Allcroft and John Kane

Published in Great Britain by World International, an imprint of Egmont Publishing Ltd.,
Egmont House, PO Box 111, Great Ducie Street, Manchester M60 3BL.
Printed in Great Britain.
ISBN 07498 2396 8

Mumfie is a special little elephant who lived all alone and had no one to play with. Every morning he would run to his letter box, thinking,

"I wonder if an adventure has arrived – all tied up in a parcel!"

After waiting a long time Mumfie decided that adventures might not come in parcels after all.

"Instead," he said, "I shall have to go out and find one."

At the edge of the woods, just beyond his little cottage, sat a bird in a bare tree.

"Where are you going?" asked the bird.

Mumfie explained and promised that when he returned, he would bring the tree a present.

So Mumfie set off, and soon made friends with a lonely Scarecrow. Together they met Pinkey, a little pink pig with wings. Pinkey was sad, she had lost her mother and longed to find her again. All Pinkey could remember was a mysterious Island.

"You can find her," comforted Mumfie. "And we're going to help you. Your Island must be in the middle of the sea, so first we must go to the seaside."

At the seaside, they discovered Whale. Whale – fitted out like a beautiful ship – was happy to have company, and sped his passengers across the water.

"Home!" cried Pinkey at last. "I can see home."

But Pinkey's Island was now a gloomy place. No singing, dancing, whistling or fun of any kind was allowed.

The beautiful Queen of Night who took care of the Island had been overpowered by her wicked Secretary and he had locked up all who lived there.

In his determination to restore happiness to the Island, Mumfie learns of the Secretary's plan to steal the Queen's jewel – 'A treasure beyond price'.

By accident, Mumfie becomes keeper of the jewel. He befriends Napoleon Jones, an old Raven and the sparkling Electric Eel.

Everywhere Mumfie went, a strange and magical Black Cat went too.

The adventures continued to unfold on land, in the sky and under the sea, with the wicked Secretary and Bristle, his bossy prison guard, always on our heroes' trail.

Along the way, Mumfie and his friends faced a band of pesky pirates, led by Captain Davy Jones, and rescued a kind Admiral from the pirate's clutches. The Admiral and his wife became firm friends of Mumfie, too.

At last goodness overcame evil; the wicked Secretary was turned into a stone inkwell; Pinkey and her mother were reunited; Bristle mended his ways and both he and the pirates became loyal to Her Majesty the Queen of Night. Davy Jones became Deck Steward on the good ship *Whale*!

"You have been trusting, kind and courageous," said the Queen to Mumfie, and she gave him her magic jewel to keep as his own.

Then Mumfie and Scarecrow said goodbye to their friends and returned home. The bird in the bare tree was waiting.

"I've brought the tree a present!" laughed Mumfie, and gently hung the jewel amongst its branches. In a matter of moments, the tree grew leaves and flowers, that shimmered and shone in the light.

"Scarecrow," whispered Mumfie. "Will you keep me company always?"

"We can have lots more adventures."

"Of course," replied Scarecrow, and that is exactly what they did.

MUMFIE'S WINTER RESCUE

It was a cold winter's morning. Scarecrow slowly opened his bedroom door.

"Brrr," he shivered. "I'd better wear warm socks today." When he was dressed, he went downstairs.

Mumfie was finishing his breakfast. As it was Monday, he was eating a large bowl of rice pudding topped with a spoonful of Mrs Admiral's homemade raspberry jam. There was plenty more for Scarecrow.

"I'll have a stick of celery, too," decided Scarecrow. "It's not so nice without celery." Mumfie didn't agree, but he was much too busy munching to say so. By the time breakfast was over, the weather was colder still.

"We need a fire in the hearth," said Scarecrow. "I'll fetch some wood."

The logs were neatly stacked at the back of Mumfie's cottage. Scarecrow gathered a big bundle into his arms. When he came indoors again, Mumfie was looking through the window. The trees and grass were covered in frost.

"Everything looks so beautiful," said Mumfie. "Let's go out before we light the fire."

Scarecrow felt an icicle dangling from his nose. "What if we freeze?" he muttered.

"We won't if we walk fast enough!" replied Mumfie.

When they had put on their hats, coats and gloves, the two friends set off through the trees. Soon they reached the beach.

"We may not be frozen," gasped Scarecrow, "but look at the sea!" The sea stretched away like a vast sheet of glass before them. Then Scarecrow noticed something else. "What is that in the distance? It looks familiar."

"It is familiar," replied Mumfie. "It's Whale!"

Scarecrow was puzzled. "If the sea has frozen over, what's Whale doing in the middle of it?"

"He must be stuck!" cried Mumfie. "We'd better get our skates on."

They hurried back to the cottage, fetched their skates, and returned to the beach. When they'd put on their skates, they stepped gingerly across the ice.

"Let's be careful," warned Scarecrow. "If the ice is thin it might break."

But Mumfie and Scarecrow are not very heavy and the ice was very thick. Soon the two friends were speeding towards Whale.

"He looks so sad," said Mumfie.

"My friends," boomed Whale. "I'm so glad to see you. I'm in a bit of a hole." His big eyes looked down at the ice. "Stuck, in fact."

"We'll help," said Scarecrow, but he didn't really know how. "When do you think the ice will melt, Mumfie?" asked Scarecrow.

"It could be days," said Mumfie. "Unless, of course, we can make it melt."

"Hmm," said Scarecrow. He paused for a moment to calm his nerves. "How could we do that, Mumfie?"

There was a long silence. Suddenly, Mumfie had an idea. "Electric Eel! She'll be able to help!"

"Of course," said Whale. "Why didn't I think of her before?"

"We must find her," said Mumfie. "Do you know where she is, Whale?"

Whale frowned. "I'm afraid not," he said. "I haven't seen her for some time."

"Then we'll find her for you," said Mumfie. "Come on, Scarecrow. Let's start looking."

When they had left Whale far behind them, Scarecrow whispered, "Where are we going, Mumfie?"

"I'm not sure," admitted Mumfie. "But I wanted Whale to think I knew. I thought it would cheer him up."

Mumfie and Scarecrow skated on, searching for a light beneath the ice that would show them Eel was in the water below. After a while, they began calling, too. "Eel, Eel!" they shouted. But there was no reply.

It began to get dark. "Perhaps we should give up," said Scarecrow, who didn't like the idea of being out at night on a frozen sea. "We could try again tomorrow."

"You may be right," said Mumfie wearily. "Let's start back."

But which was the way back? The ice stretched ahead of them as far as they could see in every direction.

"I think we're lost," muttered Scarecrow.

"No, we're not," said Mumfie. "It's just that we're not quite sure where we are."

Scarecrow thought that sounded much the same thing, but he didn't say so. He looked about him. "Let's go this way," he said.

"No, I think we should go this way," said Mumfie, pointing in the other direction.

Before they could decide, they heard a voice.

"Well, shine a light – how are you?"

Mumfie and Scarecrow spun round. "Eel!" they cried together.

"I'm glad you remember me," said Eel, poking her head up through a hole in the ice, "cos I sure haven't forgotten you."

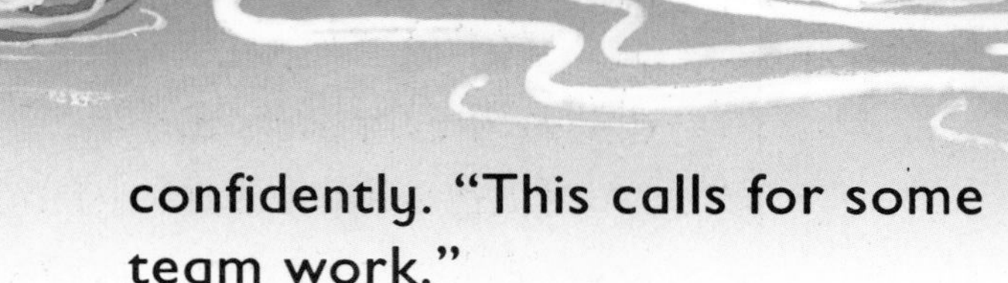

"But we've been looking for you all day," said Mumfie.

"And now you've found me," said Eel. "D'you want a little help from your friends?"

"Why, yes!" cried Mumfie. "How do you know?"

"How d'you think?" said Eel proudly, patting her bonnet with one fin. "I'm always switched on!"

"It's Whale," interrupted Scarecrow, "he's stuck in the ice."

"And you are wondering if I could melt the ice and unstick him, I suppose?" said Eel.

"That's right," replied Mumfie. "Could you?"

"Nothing simpler," replied Eel confidently. "This calls for some team work."

And, with a flick of her tail, she disappeared. Moments later, Mumfie and Scarecrow saw a trail of lights beneath the ice.

"We're ready," said Eel, popping her head up through the hole again. "Where's Whale?" Mumfie and Scarecrow stared at their skates in embarrassment.

"Erm... we don't exactly know," said Mumfie.

Eel smiled. "Then it's a good job that I think I do. Follow me."

The trail of lights set off at a cracking pace, and Mumfie and Scarecrow skated after them. Soon, the dark shape of Whale came into view. He was very happy to see them.

"Now stand well back," said Eel to Mumfie and Scarecrow. "Or you might get a shock."

Under the ice all the electric eels formed a ring around Whale.

"Are you ready, ladies? We need a lot of sparks and to do that we have to get very angry indeed."

So all the eels thought of all the things that made them feel angry, and soon there were lots of sparks. Suddenly, there was a high sizzling sound and all the ice around Whale melted. Whale gave himself a good shake.

"Free at last!" he cried. "My dear friends, you are so kind."

"Don't mention it," said Eel. "I'll see you around sometime."

And with a flick of her tail she was gone.

"What will you do now, Whale?" asked Scarecrow.

"Me?" said Whale. "Oh, I shall dive down to the bottom of the sea where the water's warmer and wait for the spring. Goodbye, and thank you," he boomed.

Mumfie and Scarecrow waved until he was out of sight. Then they skated home as fast as they could, thinking all the time of the cosy cottage and the welcoming fire that would soon keep them warm.

Mumfie's Munchies

Mumfie could only find a few biscuit crumbs to take along on his adventure. If you go on an adventure, make sure you are prepared. Here is a biscuit recipe to help you on your way!

Before you start:

Ask a grown-up to help you.
Make sure that you have everything you need to make the recipe.
Wash your hands!

Step 1.
Put the butter, sugar and vanilla into a bowl. Stand the bowl in very warm water. Mix these ingredients with a wooden spoon until the mixture is creamy.

Step 2.
Break the egg and pour it into the bowl. Make sure there is no shell in the mixture! Mix it in well using a fork.

Step 3.
Using a sieve, sift the flour into the bowl. Stir it in well, making sure that there are no lumps.

Step 4.
Tip the mixture, which should be a big doughy lump, on to a clean work surface sprinkled with flour. Knead it lightly. Now, using your rolling pin, roll it out to about 6mm thick.

Step 5.
Cut out the biscuits with your biscuit cutter. Now put them on a greased baking tray. Ask a grown-up to put it into the oven (190C/375F/Gas Mark 5). Now bake your biscuits in the oven until they are golden brown. This should take 10-15 minutes.

Step 6
Ask a grown-up to take them out of the oven. Make sure you wait for them to cool down before you take them on your adventures!

MUMFIE'S SNEEZES

(1) Mumfie and Scarecrow were staying in the Queen of Night's palace. One morning Mumfie woke up to find that – ATISHOO! – he had a cold.

(2) "TO BED!" ordered Bristle in his well meaning, but rather bossy way. "And I know just what you need! Nose streams, lemon drinks, vapour rubs..."

(3) "Or perhaps, instead, some peace and quiet," said Napoleon Jones wisely. "Not all these treatments."

"Nonsense!" cried Bristle good naturedly. "Bristle knows best."

(4) Soon Scarecrow and Napoleon found that Bristle wouldn't even let Mumfie have any visitors. He insisted on nursing him himself.

(5) "Poor Mumfie," said Scarecrow.

At last, several days later, Mumfie was declared fit and well.

"I'm glad I didn't give you any of my sneezes," he said to his friends.

(6) "But this is no surprise," said Napoleon with a shrug. "We did not see you. The only one allowed to visit was..."

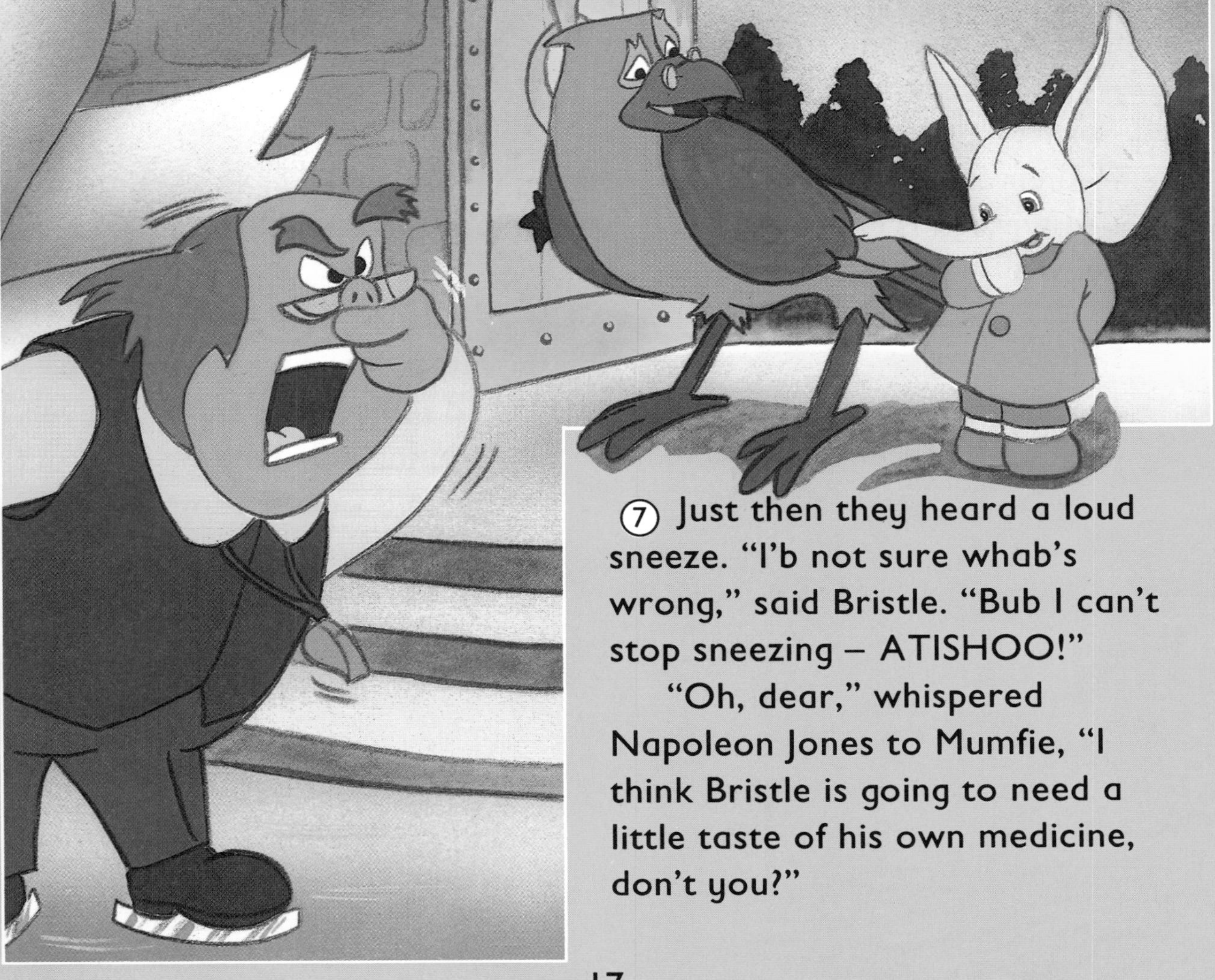

(7) Just then they heard a loud sneeze. "I'b not sure whab's wrong," said Bristle. "Bub I can't stop sneezing – ATISHOO!"

"Oh, dear," whispered Napoleon Jones to Mumfie, "I think Bristle is going to need a little taste of his own medicine, don't you?"

A FISHY TALE

One morning, when Mumfie opened his letterbox, he found a postcard inside. "Look, Scarecrow," he cried. "This is from Mrs Admiral."

"My Dears," she had written, "me and Mr Admiral were thinking that it's high time you had a little holiday at the bottom of the sea. Can you come and stay with us? Whale will wait at the beach this afternoon, and you can dive down in him. Love, Mrs Admiral."

So, that afternoon, Mumfie and Scarecrow made their way down to the beach. They were very excited at the thought of seeing their kind friends again.

Sure enough there was Whale, waiting for them at the water's edge.

"How lovely to see you," he boomed. "Climb aboard! Your holiday starts here!"

Mumfie and Scarecrow climbed up Whale's ladder and on to his back. Then they made their way down through his blow-hole.

Inside, Whale – decked out like the most beautiful luxury ship – looked more splendid than ever. Davy Jones was waiting to greet them. He'd once been a pesky pirate, but only because he was bored. Now he was Whale's busy deck steward.

"I'm glad you're still here," said Mumfie to Davy.

"Aah," said Davy, "this is a much better way to sail the high seas than that scurvy pirate business."

Whale gave a great flick of his tail and dived through the water.

Down and down he swam, while Mumfie and Scarecrow gazed out through his portholes. At last, Whale came to the seabed and laid anchor beside the Admiral's cottage. The door flew open and two familiar figures appeared.

"Mr and Mrs Admiral!" cried Mumfie.

"You haven't changed a bit," smiled Scarecrow.

"Thank you for delivering our guests, Dearie," called Mrs Admiral to Whale.

"My pleasure," boomed Whale. "Have a good holiday all

of you!"

Mr and Mrs Admiral were delighted to see their friends again. They had so much news to exchange that the evening passed fast and soon it was time for bed.

"Just think," said Mumfie to Scarecrow, as he settled down to sleep. "This morning we didn't know when we'd see the Admirals again, and now here we are in their cottage..."

"...At the bottom of the sea," finished Scarecrow, in a sleepy voice. "No cares, no worries."

It was different in the morning. "I'm at my wits' end," cried Mrs Admiral.

"What is it?" asked Scarecrow.

"Some careless swordfish swam into our roof last night and made a pesky great hole. Now we've got a leak."

"A leak?" said Scarecrow, looking puzzled. "But we're underwater."

"When you live down here Dearie," explained Mrs Admiral, "it's not water getting in you need to worry about – it's fish," and she looked around the room.

Suddenly, Mumfie and Scarecrow noticed them. Fish! They were everywhere! There were fish in the teapot, fish in the grandfather clock, fish on the lampshades... "And the bath is full of them," said Mr Admiral wearily.

"We'll try our best to help you," said Mumfie.

"Bless you, Dearie, but how?" asked Mrs Admiral.

That was the question. Everyone thought hard. Suddenly, Mr Admiral sprang to his feet. "Crabs and lobsters!" he exclaimed. "I've got an idea!" He hurried to the cupboard and started rummaging.

"...Here somewhere...sure...could've sworn..." they heard him muttering.

"What ever is it you're after, my dear?" asked Mrs Admiral.

"Here it is!" said Mr Admiral triumphantly, holding a small tube in his hand.

"What is it?" asked Mumfie.

"A music pipe," chuckled Mr Admiral. "And a special one too. It was given to me by a mermaid."

"A mermaid!" exclaimed Mrs Admiral.

"Oh, it was before I knew you, my dear," Mr Admiral reassured her.

"I didn't know there were mermaids. Did you, Scarecrow?" whispered Mumfie.

"I dunno," replied Scarecrow. "I've never been down here long enough to find out."

"It's all very well, my dear," continued Mrs Admiral to her husband, "but what's a mermaid got to do with fish?"

"She taught me a few tunes," explained Mr Admiral. "And, if I'm not very much mistaken, there's one that I can remember."

He lifted the pipe to his lips and began to play. It was a strange tune – one that neither Mumfie nor Scarecrow had ever heard before. But it had the most amazing effect.

As soon as Mr Admiral started playing, all the fish began to sway from side to side with the music. Then one by one, they came out of their hiding places and danced towards Mr Admiral.

When all the fish were gathered round, Mr Admiral slowly turned and started to walk out of the cottage, still playing his strange tune. And swaying from side to side, the fish followed him.

Mumfie and Scarecrow saw Mr Admiral stroll off across the seabed and soon there wasn't a single fish left in the house.

"Well – mermaid music. Who would have thought it?" laughed Mrs Admiral. "We'll have no more trouble with them fish, thank Neptune. But there's just one other problem..."

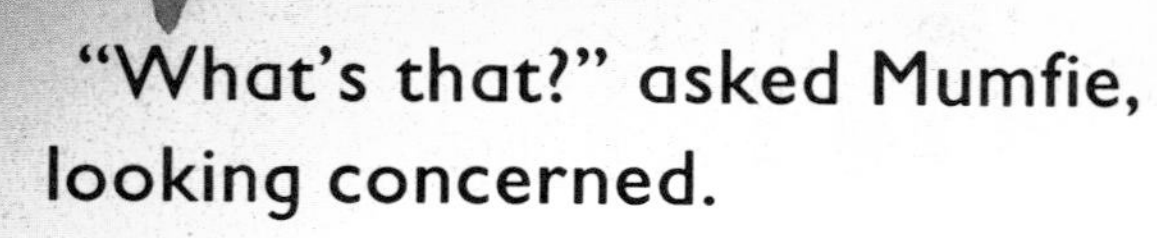

"What's that?" asked Mumfie, looking concerned.

"D'you suppose..." began Mrs Admiral, with a twinkle in her eye, "he knows a magic tune for mending a hole in the roof, too?"

Mystery Code

Mumfie has found a letter.
It is all in code! Can you help Mumfie break the code and read the letter?

The code is at the bottom of the page.

Dear Mumfie, I know where the is. Before you look for the , make sure that the isn't following you. The is very special and the will help you find it. So find the first, before you start looking for the

In gratitude, 

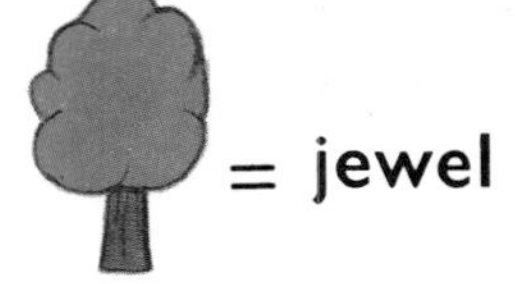 = jewel 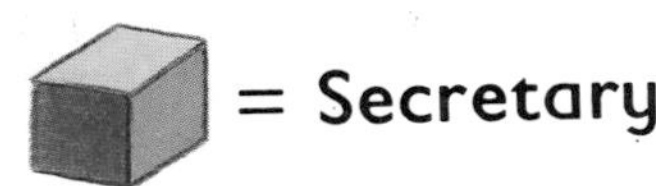 = Secretary 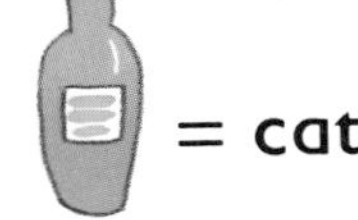 = cat  = Queen of Night

Look on page 61 for the answer.

Who am I?

Mumfie and his friends are playing a trick on you! Can you tell who is who by reading these clues?

Write the correct letter in the box next to the picture and then write their name below each one. **Good luck!**

a. I have a pink jacket, a trunk and carry a jewel in my pocket.
Who am I?

b. I am part made of wood, was found in a field and wear a hat.
Who am I?

c. I live in the ocean and because I am fitted like an ocean liner can carry passengers.
Who am I?

d. I am pink, with wings, and my mother lives on the Island.
Who am I?

e. I live in the sea and I light up, but you don't switch me on!
Who am I?

☐

_ _ _ _ _ _

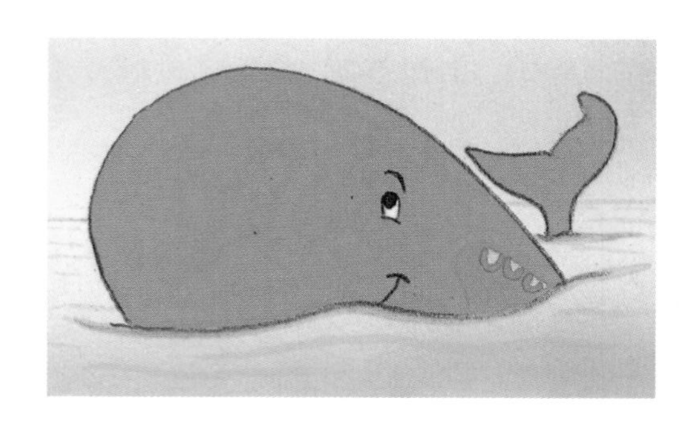

☐

_ _ _ _ _

☐

_ _ _

☐

_ _ _ _ _ _ _ _ _ _ _ _ _ _

☐

_ _ _ _ _ _

Mumfie's Muddle

What is wrong with this picture?
There are SIX things wrong with it.
Can you find them all?

PINKEY'S PROBLEM

One morning, Pinkey – the little pink pig with wings – and her mother arrived at the cottage to see Mumfie and Scarecrow.

"Take care of yourself, Pinkey," said her mother. "Don't make a mess and enjoy your holiday. I'll be back to fetch you next week."

Pinkey was very excited at the idea of a whole week, staying with her special friends.

Scarecrow tucked Pinkey under his arm, and they all waved goodbye as Pinkey's mother flew off above the trees.

"We're together again, just like old times!" squeaked Pinkey.

And what fun it was! The weather was sunny, Mumfie and Scarecrow packed up a picnic, and they all started off through the wood.

Soon they found a little clearing, and sat down to eat their picnic. When they'd finished, Pinkey said, "I know! Let's play some games. Do you know how to play tag?"

Scarecrow wasn't sure that he did, so Pinkey and Mumfie explained the game to him. Then they started. First, Pinkey chased Scarecrow and Mumfie, then Mumfie chased, and then it was Scarecrow's turn. Soon Scarecrow was out of breath. "Phew, this is a tiring game," he said.

"Can't catch me!" laughed Pinkey, flying past him as fast as she could.

Suddenly, Mumfie gasped. "Pinkey. Look out!"

But it was too late. BUMP!

Pinkey flew straight into the branch of a tree.

"Are you all right? Are you hurt?" asked Mumfie and Scarecrow anxiously.

"I-I'm fine," stammered Pinkey faintly. "At least, I think so. I just feel a bit dizzy."

"Well, that's enough fun and games for one day," said Scarecrow firmly. "Let's get you home."

Pinkey quickly recovered from her bump on the head. Soon she was chattering and laughing again, full of news of everything she'd been doing since she last saw her friends.

But there was one problem.

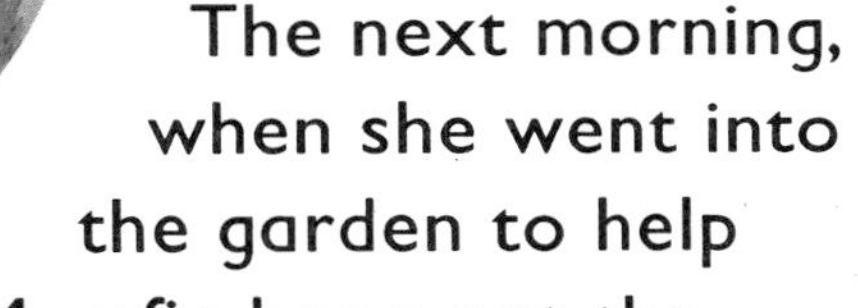

The next morning, when she went into the garden to help Mumfie hang out the washing, Pinkey discovered something very strange. She'd forgotten how to fly. She stood and flapped her wings, but nothing happened.

"How can I be a piglet with wings and forget how to fly?" she sniffed sadly. "Whatever will Mama say?"

"Don't worry, Pinkey," said Mumfie. "We'll help you remember."

All day, Mumfie and Scarecrow tried their very best to help Pinkey remember how to fly. They ran along, flapping their arms, and jumping in the air. But it was no good.

"It's because we haven't any wings ourselves," said Scarecrow glumly. "We don't know what they feel like."

Then Mumfie had an idea. "Napoleon will help," he said. Napoleon Jones is, as you may remember, an old raven who lives in the Queen of Night's palace. "When you get back to the Island, Napoleon will teach you how to fly again." Pinkey nodded sadly and sniffed a little.

To help cheer Pinkey up, Mumfie decided that they would find her plenty to do. Near the cottage there was a tree covered with beautiful shiny apples that were just ripe for picking. This gave Mumfie an idea.

"Pinkey, will you help me pick some apples?" he asked her. "Then we can make your favourite apple pie for our supper." Pinkey nodded.

With Scarecrow's help, Mumfie fetched a ladder whilst Pinkey made encouraging squeaks.

"You keep an eye on the basket, Pinkey, while I climb up to the apples," said Mumfie.

But this made Pinkey even sadder than before. She could see that the best, shiniest apples were right at the top of the tree.

"I wish I could fly up to them," she said.

"Don't worry," Mumfie reassured her. "I can reach them with the ladder."

Mumfie climbed right to the top and stretched up his trunk to the highest branches. The apples there were beautifully big and shiny, and the best apple of all was hanging from the very top branch. Mumfie stretched his trunk, but he couldn't quite reach it. So he stretched a bit more...and a bit more...too much!

He wobbled, then lost his balance and tumbled off the ladder.

Down and down he fell, bumping against branches as he went. The ground was getting closer and closer...

All at once, Mumfie felt himself land on something soft and white. It was the tablecloth that he'd hung out on the washing line to dry. Pinkey had grabbed one edge of it. Pinkey lifted it up to break Mumfie's fall. But she had done more than help Mumfie.

"Pinkey!" exclaimed Mumfie, gazing up at his friend in wonder. "You're flying!"

"My! So I am!" laughed Pinkey, flapping her wings happily.

"You've cured me!"

Just then, Scarecrow came running out of the cottage. He'd seen everything through the window.

"You did give me a shock, Mumfie," he said, hugging his friend in relief.

"Me, too," said Pinkey, "but that's just what I needed!"

"I suppose you could say, Pinkey," laughed Mumfie, "I just solved your problem by accident!"

Mystery Island Word Search

Someone's name is missing.
Do you know which one?
Find each name on the grid.
Look up and down,
backwards and forwards.

Put a tick in the box when you
have found each one.
Circle the name that is missing
from the grid.

E	D	A	V	Y	J	O	N	E	S
S	L	I	E	A	W	S	E	L	P
C	I	S	V	A	B	D	Q	A	Z
A	P	E	Z	C	A	T	U	H	V
R	I	A	L	E	L	P	E	W	A
E	N	B	R	L	E	E	E	W	E
C	K	R	K	B	N	S	N	N	O
R	E	A	B	R	I	S	T	L	E
O	Y	Z	N	I	O	W	P	Z	R
W	V	N	O	E	L	O	P	A	N

QUEEN ☐ CAT ☐ DAVY JONES ☐

WHALE ☐ PINKEY ☐ EEL ☐

MUMFIE ☐ BRISTLE ☐ SCARECROW ☐

NAPOLEON ☐

Whose name is missing? Find out on page 61.

Pirate Peril

It's a race!

Who will get to the Island first,
Mumfie or the Pirates?

Mumfie throws the die first,
and the pirates follow him.

Mumfie's squares are RED and the
Pirates' squares are BLACK.

If Mumfie lands on a black square,
he has to go back one space.

If the Pirates land on a red square,
they have to go back one space,
and so on.

If either land on a green square,
they miss a turn.

Each player takes it in turn to
throw the die.

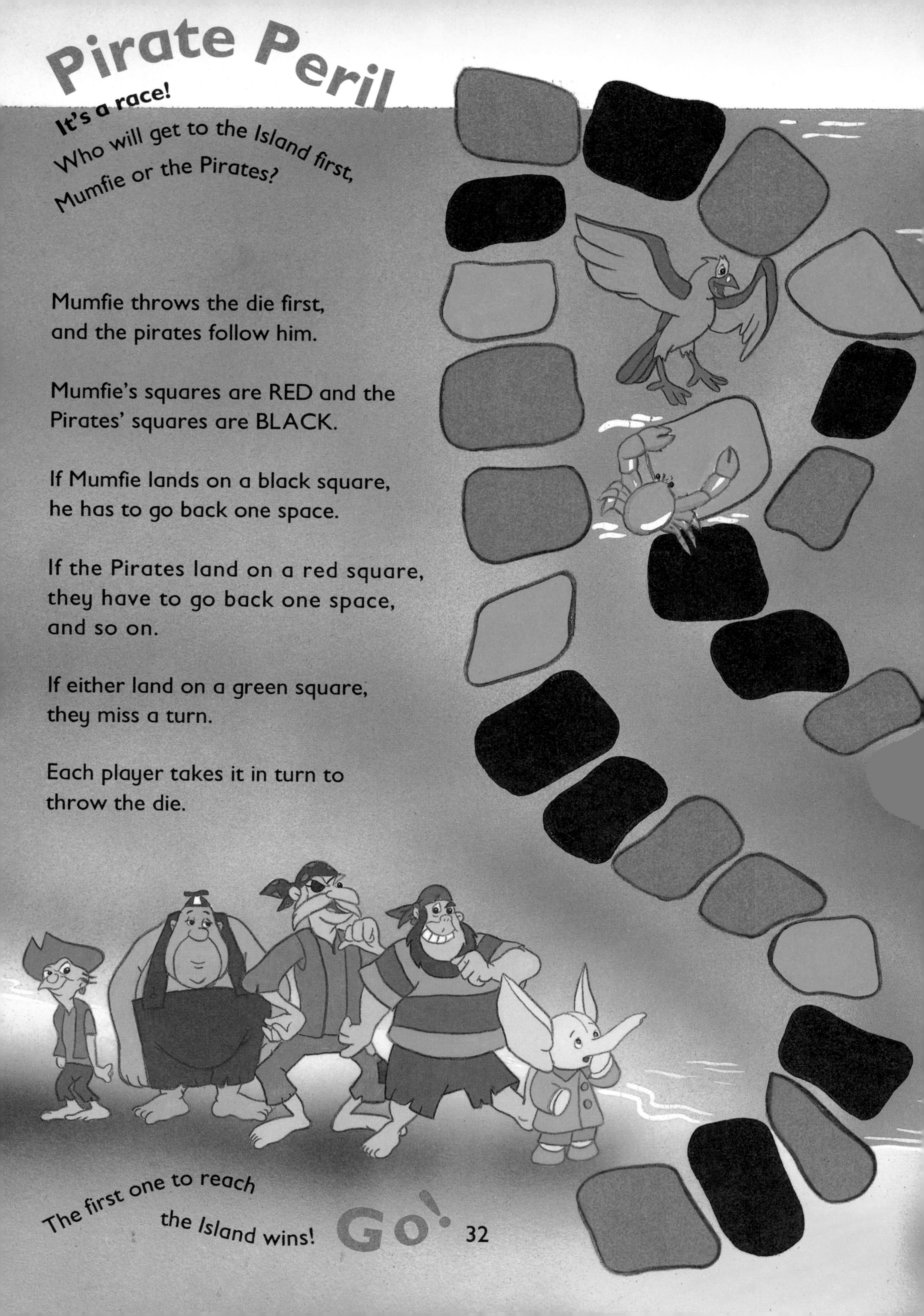

The first one to reach
the Island wins!

A PRESENT FOR THE QUEEN

One day, Mumfie and Scarecrow received a beautiful invitation.

"It's from the Queen of Night!" gasped Mumfie. "It's her birthday soon, and she's holding a party in the palace gardens."

"And we're invited?" asked Scarecrow, feeling honoured.

"Yes," said Mumfie. "We must take her a present. I wonder what it should be?"

"It'll have to be something very special," said Scarecrow.

But try as they might, Mumfie and Scarecrow couldn't think of anything that they had that was special enough to give to the Queen.

"I know," said Mumfie, at last. "Why don't we make her something?"

"But what?" asked Scarecrow

"A poem," said Mumfie. "A special birthday poem!"

This sounded like a very hard task to Scarecrow, but they set to work. For a long time they chewed their pencils, and scratched their heads, and stared out of the window, trying to think up words to rhyme with "Queen" and "birthday". It was very tricky.

Meanwhile, across the seas something was stirring. Davy Jones' cousin, Jolly Roger, was up to mischief.

Now Jolly Roger was a jolly man by nature, but he had spent all his life trying to be as pesky as his pirate cousin Davy. He didn't realize that Davy had mended his ways.

"I'm going to form a dastardly

plan," Jolly Roger sneered, trying to sound very fierce. "When Davy hears about it, he'll be really impressed!"

But what should the plan be? Then a passing pigeon, of the sea-going sort, told him about the Queen's birthday party.

"This is our chance!" Jolly Roger said to his pirate crew. "If everyone is going to some jolly...er, I mean scurvy party, in the palace gardens, who will be left to guard the Queen's treasure? We'll be able to help ourselves, me hearties!" And he laughed a nasty laugh that he'd practised specially.

At last, the day of the Queen's birthday party arrived. Scarecrow and Mumfie, wearing their smartest clothes, set off for the Island where the Queen of Night lived, as well as Pinkey, and many of their other friends, too.

They crossed the sea with the help of their friend Whale, and soon arrived at the palace gates.

There they met Bristle.

"Have you brought a present?" he snapped.

"Of course we have," laughed Mumfie.

"Where is it, then?" asked Bristle, walking right round them to see if they were hiding anything.

"Here," said Scarecrow, holding up a piece of paper. "It's a poem."

"And we are going to perform it for the Queen ourselves," added Mumfie.

In the palace gardens, everything was beautifully decorated. The Queen herself graciously greeted her guests. Napoleon Jones, Pinkey and her mother were very happy to see Mumfie and Scarecrow, too.

But after a little while, Scarecrow started looking worried.

"What is it ?" asked Mumfie.

"I'm nervous about performing our poem," said Scarecrow.

"So am I," admitted Mumfie. "Why don't we go into the palace to practise it?"

"Good idea," agreed Scarecrow.

Inside the palace, Scarecrow opened up the piece of paper and cleared his throat.

"Hush!" said Mumfie suddenly. "What was that?"

"Me, clearing my throat," said Scarecrow, and he cleared it again, just to make sure.

"No," whispered Mumfie. "I heard something else. Follow me."

Mumfie crept up to the door and peered round it. There he saw the most amazing sight.

Jolly Roger and his pirate pals were loading paintings, ornaments and precious jewels into their sacks, and laughing nasty laughs as they did so.

"Pirates!" exclaimed Scarecrow in surprise, rather louder than he meant to. Jolly Roger heard him and turned around.

"Gosh...er, cutlasses 'n' custard!" cried Jolly Roger, trying not to look frightened. "We've been spotted. Leg it, me hearties!"

The pirates grabbed their sacks, and rushed off along the corridor.

"Quick – the carpet!" said Mumfie. He and Scarecrow lifted the end of the long red palace carpet, and pulled it as hard as they could.

"Whoooaaaa!" yelled the pirates, flying in all directions. They landed in a messy heap, their bags of loot on top of them.

A little while later, in the palace garden...

"....And so this is why we want to say, Dear Queen of Night, Happy Birthday!"

Everyone cheered and clapped as Mumfie and Scarecrow finished the poem and took their bows.

"What a lovely birthday present!" said the Queen.

Mumfie and Scarecrow blushed with pleasure. Then Mumfie remembered something.

"As well as our poem, Your Majesty," he said, "we've brought you some extra presents. They're over there," and he pointed to Jolly Roger and his men, neatly rolled up in a red carpet.

"I think, Your Majesty," declared Napoleon, "we might call them, er, what shall we say – a captive audience?"

Just then, Davy Jones, who was one of the party guests, stepped forward.

"Davy Jones!" gasped Jolly Roger. "What are you doing here? I thought you were the terror of the high seas!"

Davy Jones shook his head. "That was a long time ago," he said sternly. "I know better now. And so should you."

To everyone's surprise, Jolly Roger laughed. "You mean I can stop being a pesky pirate? Shiver me timbers, what a relief! All that sailing was making me seasick!"

17 SUPER PRIZES TO BE WON!

1st PRIZE WINNER
receives one large, wonderfully soft and cuddly Mumfie
from Gund UK Ltd

NEXT 6 PRIZE WINNERS
each receive one high quality plush toy: Mumfie, Pinkey or Scarecrow
from Gund UK Ltd

NEXT 10 PRIZE WINNERS
each receive a Mumfie playset, containing jointed and non-jointed toys of all the favourite Mumfie characters,
from Hornby

HOW TO ENTER

It's easy! All you have to do is answer this simple question:

What colour are the buttons on Mumfie's coat?

Write the answer on a postcard or envelope, with your name, age and address.

Send to:
Mumfie Competition, Marketing Department, Egmont Publishing, PO Box III, Great Ducie Street, Manchester M60 3BL.

Closing date: Ist February 1996.

The first I7 correct entries selected at random after the closing date will win a prize.

RULES
Employees of World International or their respective agents may not enter this competition. The Editor's decision is final and no correspondence will be entered into. A list of winners' names will be available on request and on receipt of a SAE after I4th February 1996. The Publishers reserve the right to vary the prizes, subject to availability at the time of judging the competition.

COMPETITION

Tell Me a Story!

This is the story of Mumfie. But the order of events are jumbled up. Can you put them in the right order?

① One day Mumfie took the penny out of his money box, wrapped some cake crumbs carefully in his best handkerchief and set off into the woods.

② Mumfie, Scarecrow and Pinkey wondered how they would reach the island. "Climb aboard and I'll take you myself!" said Whale. Their adventure had begun!

③ Mumfie and Scarecrow found Pinkey in a haystack. She told them that her mother was on an Island in the middle of the sea. "You can find her," said Mumfie. "And we're going to help you do it."

④ Mumfie met Scarecrow. He gave him some cake crumbs. "I think we'd better go now," said Mumfie. "Go with you – but I haven't moved in ages!" said Scarecrow.

Flag Fashion

The Pirates have a **'Jolly Roger'** flag flying from their mast.
Why don't you design your own flag?

Mumfie has designed one, too.
He has drawn a picture of himself.
Now, think of all the things that you like and design your own flag. When you have finished, cut it out carefully, and put in on your wall.

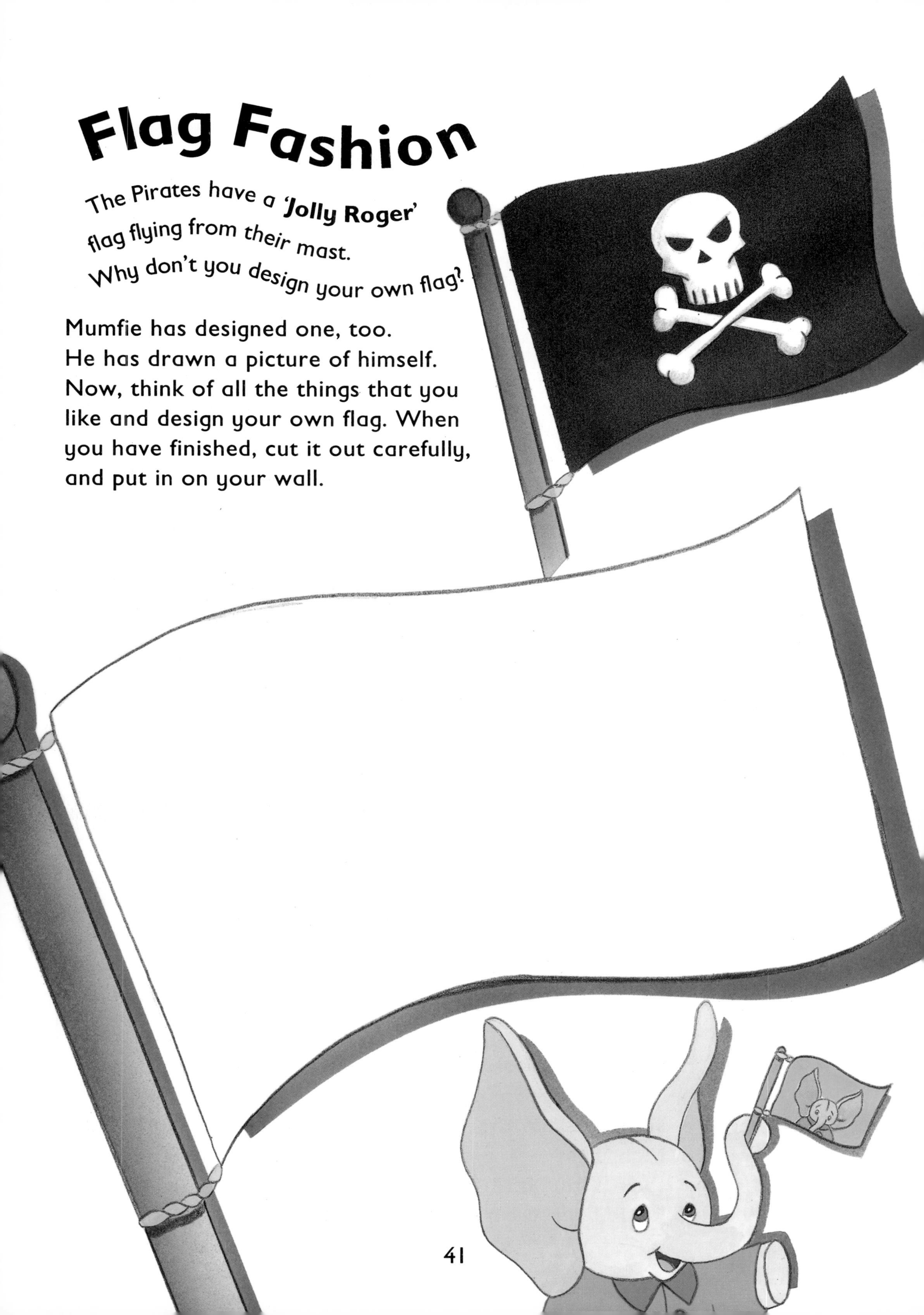

THE LONELY LIGHTHOUSE KEEPER

① Whale was taking Mumfie and Scarecrow on a special journey to the seabed to visit their good friends Mr and Mrs Admiral.

② "I remember," said Scarecrow, "that I once met a lighthouse keeper who lived not far from here."

③ "Why don't we go and look for him?" suggested Mumfie. So the two friends set off across the sands. Soon, a bright light beamed across their path. "It's the lighthouse," cried Scarecrow.

④ He suddenly felt rather nervous, so Mumfie knocked on the door. But there was no need to worry. The lighthouse keeper was very friendly.

⑤ "How are you?" asked Scarecrow. "Lonely," said the keeper. "Very, very lonely. I have no visitors, no one comes to see me, no sharks, no nothing." "Why don't you go and visit someone, instead?" asked Mumfie.

⑥ The keeper looked wistful. "I'd like to visit my brothers," he said. "They have a cafe on the other side of the seabed."

⑦ "But I can't – there's no one to look after the lighthouse." At that moment, Mumfie and Scarecrow had the same idea. "We'll look after it!" they cried.

⑧ Soon, the two friends were waving goodbye to the lighthouse keeper as he set off to see his brothers.

⑨ For the next two days, Mumfie and Scarecrow stayed in the lighthouse. It was a rather dreary place. They cleaned the big light, and they played I-Spy.

⑩ But they heard no knock at the door or ring of the door bell, and there were no visitors at all. They began to see how the lighthouse keeper had become so miserable.

⑪ A few days later, the lighthouse keeper came home. "I don't expect he's happy to be back," said Scarecrow.

⑫ But to Mumfie and Scarecrow's surprise, the keeper seemed very happy indeed. "I have a magnificent plan to bring more visitors to the lighthouse," he said.

⑬ "<u>The lighthouse souvenir shop and cafe,</u>" read Mumfie. "And you see who's going to help me run it," said the keeper happily. "My brothers Flopsami and Jepsamo."

⑭ Then it was time for Mumfie and Scarecrow to leave. All the brothers were already hard at work, and the lighthouse was looking very bright and cheerful.

⑮ "I have a present for you," said the keeper. As a souvenir of their visit, the lighthouse keeper handed Mumfie and Scarecrow a little model of the lighthouse.

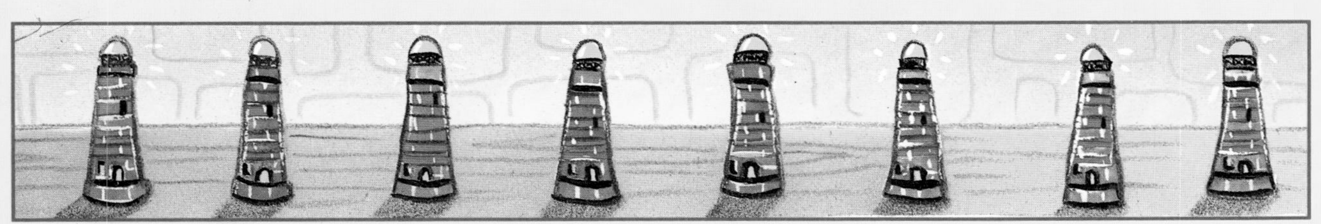

⑯ "It's lovely!" exclaimed Mumfie. "Thank you," said Scarecrow. "Ah, it's nothing," said the keeper. "I've got one or two more of them in my shop!"

Whales - Great Creatures of the Sea

The whale has lots of relations. Some are big and some are much smaller, while some types have teeth and others do not. Dolphins and porpoises belong to the whale family, too.

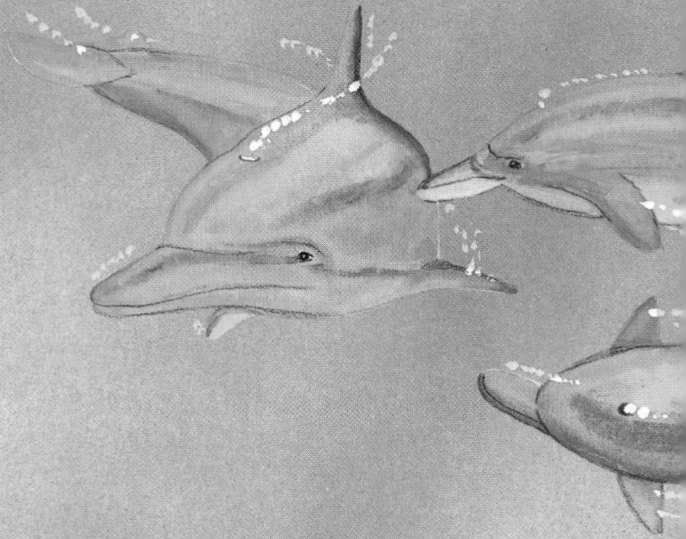

Mumfie and his friends were very lucky to meet such an unusual and helpful whale. Most whales are not fitted out like ocean liners, but they are still very interesting creatures.

As you can see, whales are indeed the greatest creatures of the sea!

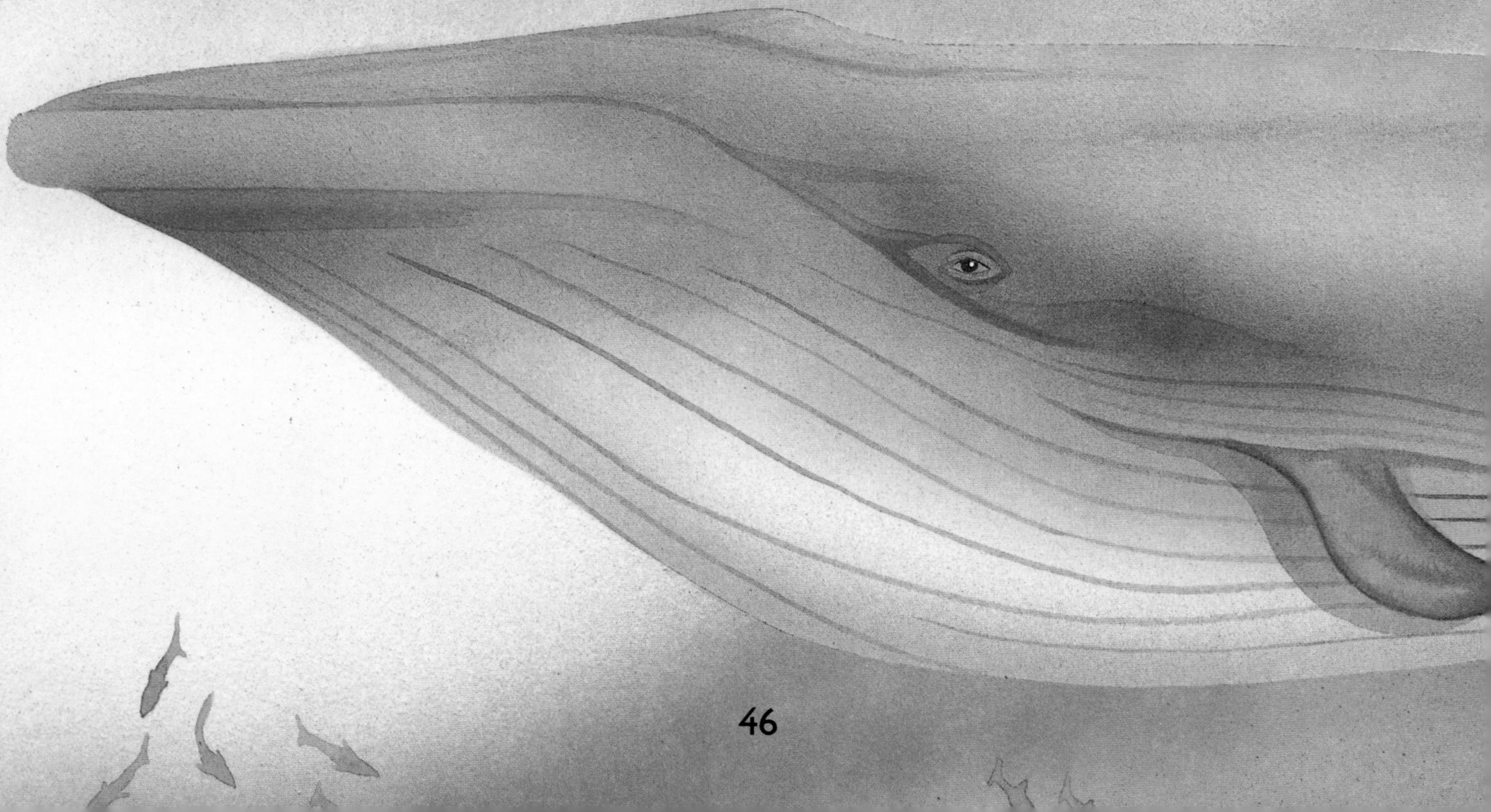

The Blue Whale is the biggest animal to have ever lived – it is even bigger than the largest dinosaur. Although the Blue Whale is huge, it eats only very tiny creatures called 'krill'. Krill are small shrimp-like creatures that live in the sea.

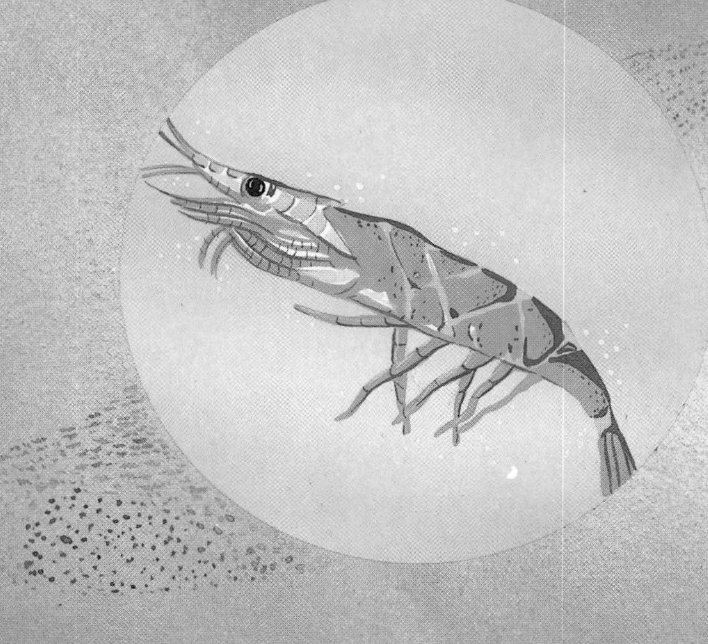

Although whales live under the sea, they have to breathe like you. They do not breathe through a nose on the front of their face but through an opening at the top of their head. The opening or hole is called a 'blow hole'. When a whale wants to breathe, it has to swim up to the surface of the water and breathe in fresh air. If it does not, it will drown. Whales do not breathe as often as you do because they can hold their breath for up to one hour.

Napoleon's French Lesson

"I say 'Bonjour!' and you say 'Hello!'. Bonjour is French for hello. I speak French because I used to live in France. Did you know that there are lots of different languages? People speak different languages in different countries. Here are some French words that you might like to learn. You say 'Goodbye!' and I say 'Au revoir!'."

English	French	Pronounce like this
cat	le chat	(ler shah)
biscuits	les biscuits	(les beece-kwee)
elephant	l'elephant	(laylayfon)
jacket	la veste	(lah vest)
pig	le cochon	(ler coh-shon)
scarecrow	l'epouvantail	(lay-poo-van-tie)
whale	la baleine	(lah bahlenn)

Au revoir!

Maze
Help Mumfie find the jewel!
Be careful not to get caught by
the Secretary or the Pirates.
Good luck!

MUMFIE'S SPRING CLEAN

The birds were singing and it was a lovely day. Mumfie woke up and lifted his trunk from under the bedclothes.

"Hmm," he sniffed happily. "I can smell Spring." He jumped out of bed, got dressed, and rushed downstairs to find Scarecrow.

"Scarecrow, Scarecrow, Spring is here!" he cried happily. "That means it's time for us to spring clean!"

"Right," said Scarecrow carefully. He'd never been asked to spring clean before and he wasn't quite sure what to do.

Then Mumfie explained, and they both set to work, dusting, polishing, sweeping, turning out cupboards and drawers, and making the little cottage sparkle from top to bottom.

Because he was taller than Mumfie, one of Scarecrow's jobs was to clean the chimney.

Mumfie gave him a long brush and he started sweeping.

Soon Scarecrow was covered in soot from head to toe. Suddenly, just as he poked his long brush right to the top of the chimney, he heard a loud squawk.

"What was that?" asked Mumfie

"I'm not sure," said Scarecrow, shaking a shower of soot from his sleeve. "But I hope it doesn't happen again."

A moment later there was an angry tapping at the window. Two grumpy-looking birds were fluttering outside.

"You've broken our nest!" they squawked at Scarecrow, and held up what looked like two halves of a messy pile of twigs.

"We were sitting in it on the top of the chimney, minding our own business, when all of a sudden – bam! – you break it in half."

"I'm very sorry," said Scarecrow. "I didn't mean to."

"Mean to or not, our nest's broken," said the birds crossly. "What are you going to do about it?"

Mumfie secretly thought that anyone so bad-tempered didn't deserve to be helped at all. But he was sorry about the nest, too, so he looked around to try and find something the birds could sit in. "You could use this," he suggested, holding up a teapot. "Or this?" He offered them a basket.

"No good," said the birds, shaking their heads. Then one of them said, "But that would do very well."

Mumfie followed the bird's gaze. "Not..." he began.

"MY HAT?" finished Scarecrow, taking it off his head.

"That's right," said the birds. Scarecrow was very fond of his hat. He dearly wanted to keep it. But he did feel bad about breaking the birds' nest.

He opened the window. "Here," he said to the birds. "You can have it."

"I should think so, too," was the rude reply, and they flew off, holding the hat in their beaks.

"Cheer up, Scarecrow," said Mumfie. "Why don't we make you a new hat?"

So, while Scarecrow had a wash to get rid of all the chimney soot, Mumfie brought out a large box. Inside were lots of scraps of bright material that he'd collected and saved.

"You can choose whatever you like," he said to Scarecrow.

Neither Mumfie nor Scarecrow had ever made a hat before, and they had several goes...

"You know, Mumfie," said Scarecrow at last, "I never thought I'd like any hat as much as my old one, but this last one is perfect."

Just then, the birds appeared at the window again.

"Your old hat's too small," they squawked. "Now you can have it back, it's all wrong for us."

"But just right for me," sighed Scarecrow happily, and he popped his old hat back on his head.

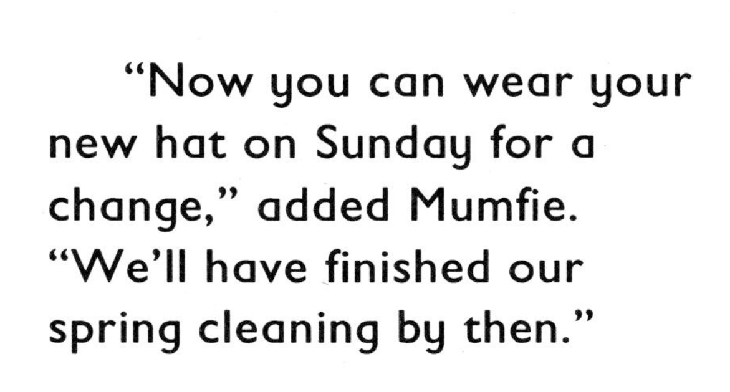

"Now you can wear your new hat on Sunday for a change," added Mumfie. "We'll have finished our spring cleaning by then."

Lock it Up!

Mumfie and his friends face lots of dangers on their adventures. There are lots of dangerous things around you, too.
Here are some pictures of everyday objects. Some are safe and some can be dangerous.

Do you know which is which?
Draw a key in the box next to each picture you think should be locked away, and a tick in the box next to the picture that is safe.
Ask a grown-up to help you.

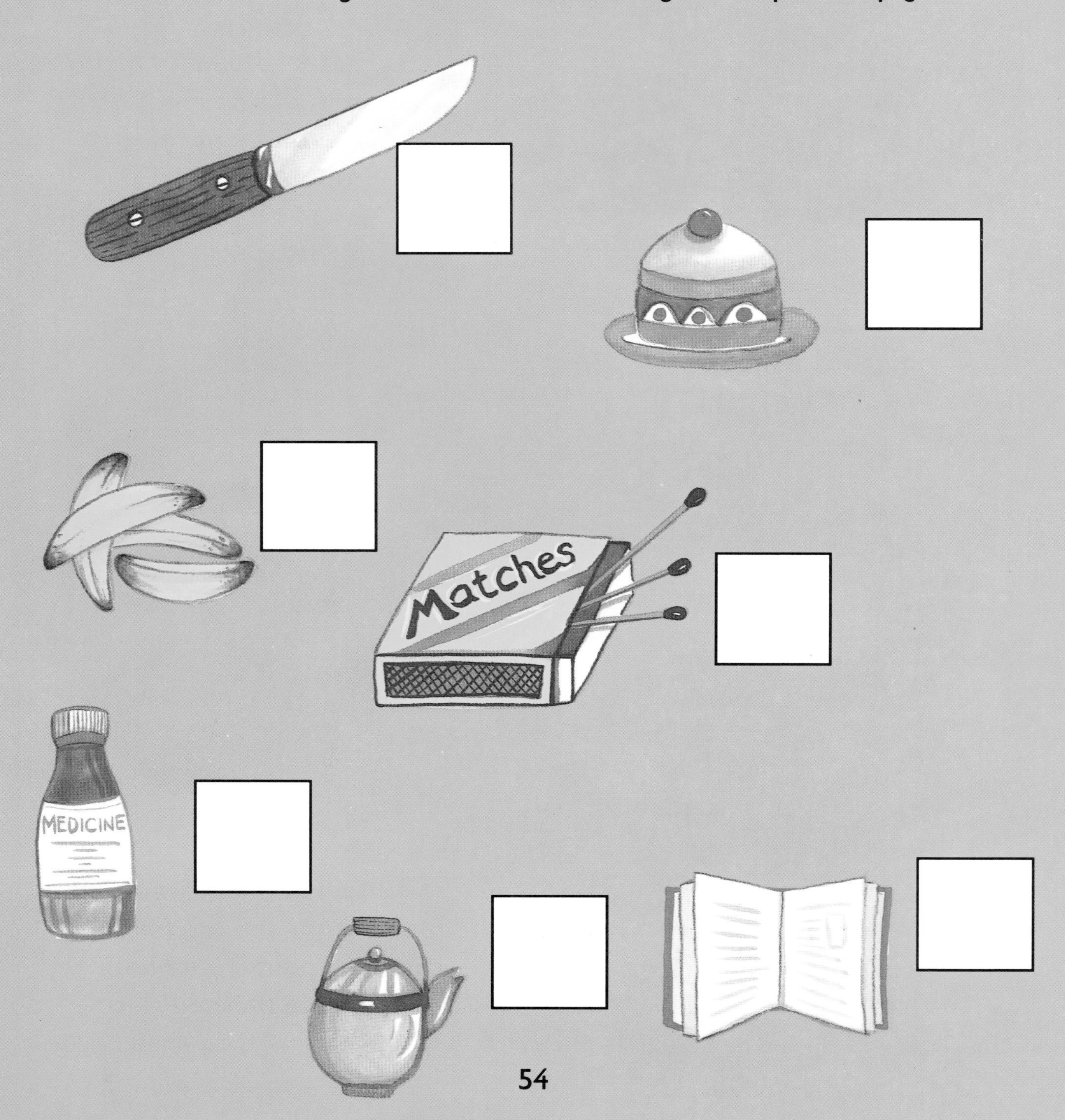

Bristle's Memory Game

"Look carefully at the pictures on this page.
Now close the book.
How many of the objects can you remember? Say them out loud.
No peeping!"

MUMFIE'S MAGIC RAINBOW

One afternoon, Mumfie and Scarecrow were playing catch in the Queen of Night's palace gardens. Mumfie was very good at the game, and caught the ball every time in his trunk. But Scarecrow was a bit of what Mumfie called a "butterfingers". The ball just seemed to slip through his fingers.

"Whooa!" cried Scarecrow as the ball sailed over his head. He staggered backwards and collided with the stone inkwell. His hat fell over this eyes.

"Where's that ball gone?" he muttered. "Ouch!" It had bounced on top of the inkwell and hit him on the head.

"Are you all right?" asked Mumfie anxiously.

"No bits broken," said Scarecrow. "But I'm not sure about this inkwell." He pointed to a crack in the stone.

Mumfie looked worried. "The Queens's magic turned the wicked Secretary into this inkwell," he said. "I hope the crack can't mess up her magic."

Soon Mumfie and Scarecrow were playing happily once more. They were enjoying themselves so much that they forgot all about the inkwell. But that night, there was a terrible storm. Mumfie and Scarecrow huddled close to one another at their window. All of a sudden Mumfie gasped.

"What's that?" he whispered, pointing up into the sky. A sinister black shape was rising high into the air.

"It looks just like..." began Mumfie.

"... The wicked Secretary!" gasped Scarecrow. "Mumfie, do you think that the crack in the inkwell could have brought him back?"

Mumfie thought perhaps it could, but he didn't want to say so. Instead, he said, "Let's go and find Napoleon Jones. He'll know what to do."

So Mumfie and Scarecrow knocked on Napoleon's door. The old raven answered it straight away. "Ah, it is you, my friends," he said. "Like me, you cannot sleep. Come in, come in."

Mumfie and Scarecrow told Napoleon their fears. "This is serious indeed," he said. "We must act without delay."

"Should we wake the Queen?" asked Scarecrow.

"I fear there is no time to tell Her Majesty," said Napoleon. "We must fly after the Secretary ourselves."

Mumfie and Scarecrow climbed on to Napoleon's back. Scarecrow was worried. "What if we catch up with the Secretary?" he said. "How will we capture him?"

"Don't worry," said Mumfie firmly. "We'll think of something."

Then Napoleon flapped his wings and flew out through the open window. The wind was very fierce. "Hold tight!" called Napoleon.

The black shape grew nearer and nearer. Then suddenly there was a bright flash and a loud bang.

"W-What was that?" asked Mumfie.

Napoleon began to laugh. "Mon amis!" he exclaimed. "My friends, it was not the Secretary after all! The black shape that we saw is over there." Then just ahead of them, drifting away on the wind, Mumfie and Scarecrow saw a small dark thundercloud.

Soon the strong wind had blown the storm cloud away. In its place was the most beautiful rainbow. Mumfie and Scarecrow stared at it in wonder. They saw the most beautiful colours imaginable.

Napoleon swooped downwards. "Where are we going?" asked Mumfie.

"To the end of the rainbow!" called Napoleon. "There, you always find something good."

All at once, the three friends flew through a cloud of shimmering light and found themselves back in the palace gardens.

"Look!" cried Mumfie. The Queen of Night was swirling her beautiful magic cloak of dreams around the inkwell. Before their eyes, the crack closed up and disappeared.

"The Secretary will never return," declared Napoleon. "For as long as there are rainbows."

Mumfie's Secret Box

Mumfie has a secret box to keep the jewel and thimble safe. Why don't you make a secret box to keep your jewellery (or very secret things) in one place.

You will need:
small box with a lid, shiny card or paper foil, glitter, non-toxic paper, glue, safety scissors, cotton wool or shredded tissue paper

1. Cut interesting shapes out of the shiny card or foil and stick them on to your box.

2. Spell your name with the glue, or the name of the person you will be giving your secret box to, on the lid of the box. Sprinkle the glitter over the glue.

3. Put cotton wool or shredded tissue paper inside the box.

4. Your secret box is finished! What will you put in yours?

Answers

Page 23 Mystery Code

Dear Mumfie, I know where the **jewel** is. Before you look for the **jewel**, make sure that the **Secretary** isn't following you. The **jewel** is very special and the **cat** will help you find it. So, find the **cat** before you look for the **jewel**. In gratitude, **Queen of Night**.

Page 24 Who am I?

a. Mumfie, **b.** Scarecrow, **c.** Whale, **d.** Pinkey, **e.** Eel.

Page 25

Mumfie's Muddle

Mumfie is wearing Scarecrow's hat, Pinkey is flying upside down, Napoleon Jones is blue instead of grey, the black cat has two tails, Whale is out of the water and Mr Admiral has a trunk instead of a nose!

Page 31

Mystery Island Word Search

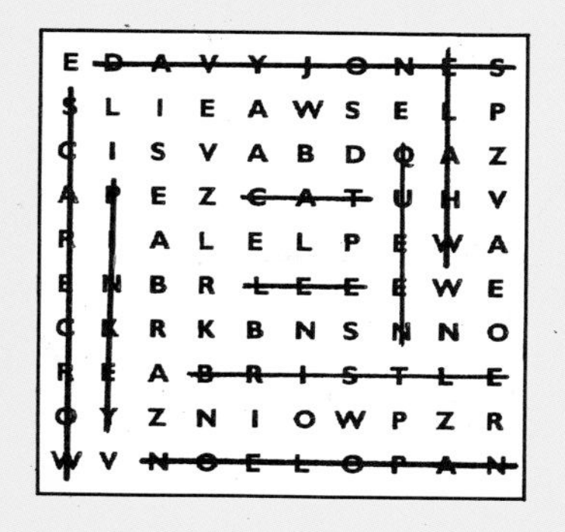

Mumfie is missing.

Page 40

Tell Me a Story!

The pictures should have been in this order: **1, 4, 3, 2.**

Page 54 Lock it Up!

The pictures of things that can be dangerous are: knife, box of matches, medicine bottle and boiling kettle. Can you think of anything in your home that might be dangerous?